AJASA

ELIZABETH EMEJUAIWE

ISBN 979-8-88943-703-1 (paperback)
ISBN 979-8-88943-704-8 (digital)

Christian Faith Publishing
832 Park Avenue
Meadville, PA 16335
www.christianfaithpublishing.com

Printed in the United States of America

Acknowledgments

This book is dedicated to my sweet Jesus, my source, the one who knit the stories together and has made this dream a reality. To my nuclear and extended family whose lives I have had the privilege of observing and continue to observe. To my parents who raised me to love and fear the lord, especially to my son, Chikamso, who quietly observed as I wrote this book. I appreciate Diane Giuffre, my literary agent, who kept on checking on me and inspiring me to move forward with my writing. Thank you, Christian Faith Publishing, for reviewing and finding my book eligible for release and for the wonderful staff at CFP led by Shante Grey who worked tirelessly to bring this miracle to life.

Ajasa

Ajasa woke up, and the peace of God filled her heart. She lifted her hands in thanksgiving. She joined her husband in America after six years of waiting in Nigeria. She arrived at George Bush Intercontinental Airport in Houston and was met by her husband, Tunde. They joyfully embraced and drove home. She started her physical marital journey wholeheartedly, doing her best to be supportive of her husband as much as possible. She would quickly realize that hers is different from her sister Tobi's and brother-in-law Kachi, where she spent all those years in her home country. No two marriages are the same.

Days rolled into months as they went through the vicissitudes of life as a couple. Ajasa noticed her husband always complained about life in the United States of America. "The people here are not as nice and warm as they show in movies." You have to just know that he'd go like that, and the reality demystified all the beauty she hoped for. Of course, there were also good roads, constant light supply, and so forth. She was favored though as her green card came three months after her arrival, and there was a nice job offer for Tunde. They moved to a nice and quiet home in the countryside. When they packed up and set out, they waved goodbye to a lovely couple who made her feel welcome.

Now Ajasa settling down in the country would also entail writing some exams and getting a job and a driver's license. These are necessities to be a supportive wife and to get through the day-to-day challenges of this new country. Tunde had to handle bills and teach his wife how to drive. It stressed him out. She knew this was a season, and things will get better, although she didn't know when. As they worked toward getting her nursing license, her faith spiraled upward. In November of that year, her credentials were approved, and she excelled at the online exam. She also joined a community church where she enjoyed worship and continued to pray for all the Lord had provided her as a new immigrant. She went on a long ride with her husband for a process called thumb printing for the board of nursing. She welcomed the new year with trust that the uncertainties will be taken care of by the Lord who has brought her this far as they continue to do their part.

In January, the couple went on a vacation to see Ajasa's sister-in-law's family, and there her exam authorization came too. They had a nice time with Tomisi and Maduka, an excellent couple indeed, with their lovely kids. As the four-day holiday ended, they bid them good-bye, and they returned home. Ajasa sat for her exam in February but didn't make it. She drew strength from prayers and spiritual songs. Regrouped, Tomisi and her husband talked and were able to get some other study materials for dear Ajasa. It wasn't easy, but that light of hope was alive in her. Her husband and her friend Wumi were also instrumental. Wumi passed her board exam in August last year.

Ajasa had to tweak her study style a bit and reverted to using the library which had always worked well for her in her home country. It's just good to know what works for you. Luckily, there was one close to their residence. Tomisi, Tobi, Doyin, Wumi, Onyii, and her husband, Tunde, with her mother, were the encouragement team. It all paid off, as she passed the next one, and it really helped this new home.

Now came the driving exam. Ajasa had to show the state she was fit to hold a license. She started practicing intensively. She visited her sister-in-law, Tomisi, again. Her mother-in-law, Bisi, was present too. She had a nice time and was blessed with gifts. When it was time for her to head back home, Mommy Ayo, her mother-in-law's friend, came to visit too. Mommy Ayo also gave her gifts. All the monetary gifts went into paying for a driving school. She got a tough instructor who was just perfect because she knew just how to help her get to where she needed to be. Ajasa had to pray for the fear of driving away because there was no way around it. She could take cabs, buses, and *Keke* in her home country, Nigeria, but not here. Even though Uber was expensive, God came through and never let her down. Her exam day to drive a distance with a licensed examiner in the car came, and she excelled. Another great victory. Thank you, Lord. Attagirl!

Now with a nursing license and driver's license in hand, Tunde helped his wife by giving her a good template to type up a very detailed resume showing all the nursing assignments she did back home. Ajasa very quickly got phone screen interview dates as she posted her resume. It was all new, but she had her faith which she held so strong. The screen interviews went as well as a new immigrant could pull off with her faith. It led to an in-person interview where she landed her first job in the States. Her husband had got her a very nice formal shirt and a white-striped black and black jacket while she purchased nice black pants to match. The manager and staff who interviewed her asked her various questions and purposed to give her a chance. It was an enlightening experience. Though she wasn't taken after the probation period. She had gained her first experience as a nurse in a new country. She learned so many skills from the first day she set her mind to learn and serve her patients with the same fervor and compassion, which led her down this nursing path in the first place.

All things work together for good to them
who love the Lord. (Romans 8:28)

Onyinye

"Onyiiii, Onyiii!" screamed her mother from the adjoining backyard. She had gone out to spend time at her neighbor's, and it was getting late now. It's time to set up for dinner. Nkoli was keeping a close eye on her as she was now a teenager and had started being friends with Adanna, the neighbor's daughter. Nkoli just had this nagging bad feeling about the friendship.

Onyii finally came home and got a real dose of talking-to by her mother. They both prepared the meal with the help of Ike, her son, who got back from playing ball, washed up, and came to help out in the kitchen. They both knew Nkolis' mantra, "If you will eat it, be part of making it." They both took turns in washing the dishes after their meal. It was Ike's turn today. As Chima turned off his car engine, Onyii ran to him, giving him the full details of her day. Ike was in quick pursuit as he also narrated the highs and the lows of his day to his dad. They shared such a lovely family bond.

After dinner, Ike did his chore, Chima led his family in prayers, and once the lights were out in both children's rooms, Nkoli had her husband's ears, and she had a great deal to discuss. Her major concern was their daughter Onyinye. She complained about her new friend Ada and the need for them to fill up her spare time with some other gainful activities. Chima knew his wife so well not to argue or downplay her concerns. They were legitimate and so fully concurred with whatever change of routine she had planned for their daughter.

As Nkoli had her husband's full backing, she was all out to implement. She called the piano teacher and scheduled Onyinye for extra home piano lessons after school. She wasn't bothered about Ike's long basketball hours. The court was right in front of their house, so she always knew where her son was. She wasn't going to raise a daughter for seventeen years and lose her to waywardness, teenage pregnancy, or drugs, so tighten the reins she did. She also ensured her children attended church and urged them to join service units. She joined the Pray for Your Teens Women Group and was really fervent. She didn't know it all, but she had vowed to do the best she knew how for her children.

She made it a rule that her children visit the library every weekend. That meant no ball day for Ike. They picked out two books and read and discussed them at the meal table the next week. Nkoli constantly talked to her children about unprofitable friends. She encouraged them to run from friends who encourage them to be part of vices because once they led them into that path, there was no meaningful future there. It's all losses, no gains. Adanna missed her new friend and moved on when she hardly ever had any spare time.

The long-awaited day came, and it was the day Onyinye was scheduled to resume college. She would be living at the hostel. Her parents and Ike went with her to drop her off. Of course, Nkoli walked her into her room despite Onyii's plea not to bother. With one look at her roommate, she knew she had to intensify her prayers. She might be wrong, as the regular saying goes, "Don't judge a book by its cover." They stalled and stalled and had lunch at a good restaurant in the college complex. They had been here a couple of times for the school tour and to make inquiries. They had to say their goodbyes because it was a long drive home.

Nkoli couldn't hold back tears as her husband rode them home. She remembered when she gave birth to her daughter and all the roller-coaster parenting had brought. She played a song on the car DVD to keep her uplifted. Chima comforted her. Ike had already put his earpiece on and was listening to a song of his choice, leaving his parents to enjoy their partial empty-nester phase. He would be leaving for college too next year.

Onyinye had all the freedom she craved and quickly filled it with the help of her roommate, Zee. She was as wild as they come. They partied. Zee and her friends smoked while Onyii stayed out of it. She took a little alcohol but not enough to get her drunk. Onyinye never missed her classes. She was a sociology major. She always heard her mother's voice in her head. "Sweetie, trust me. Your choices every day will either lead you to a life of success or of utter failure. Choose right. The ball is in your court." She would also say "Onyii, it is when you have arrived at your zenith of success that you will have all those good things you desire. Study hard. Good looks are good, but there is more to life. Don't lead with it. Keep your eyes on Jesus. Let him lead you by the hand. He knows the way."

Onyinye also remembered her dear father, who believed in her so much. He never stopped making boast of his daughter. He would say, "There are daughters, but mine is the best." He always called her his priceless gift from God.

She knew she couldn't let her brother down too, her brother who always asked her girl questions, "Onyii, but why are girls pretty sensitive?"

And her reply would be, "Ike, quit making girls sound like toys. If you have broken any of those sweet girls' hearts, you will have me to answer. Boys are sensitive too. It shows a person is emotionally healthy."

The first semester was almost rounding up, and Zee was really struggling with her low grades. Onyinye kept encouraging her. She was soaring. Of course, she was swayed a bit by the peer pressure, but it didn't swallow her up. She just had so much right words to navigate the right turns. She had this boy named Leo from her group project coming close to being her date. They enjoyed time together, but Onyinye was mostly at the library. Now exams were closer, and she had this senior colleague named Paula who invited her to a Christian book club. This helped her move away from Zee and her friends. The book club helped her locate a good church to start attending. When Nkoli heard this on one of her numerous calls to her daughter, she screamed for joy. "Onyii, I am so proud of the woman you are becoming," she said, and as always, she said a prayer before she ended the call. Immediately after the call, Nkoli called her prayer partner, Theresa, to rejoice with her that the Lord has answered their prayers for her dear daughter.

The long-awaited exams came, and Onyii excelled with flying colors. She packed up her things and said her goodbyes. Zee didn't do so well, but the help from Onyinye helped her regroup and get it together later in the school year. They rubbed off on each other in many ways. They hugged and shared some tears. "See you next semester," said the girls.

Onyinye drove off. She had to leave early on her parents' insistence so she would be home before the traffic got unbearable. Her ride home was also a moment of reflection. She had soft rock playing, and she laughed out loud as she imagined the horrid look on her mother's face if she ever told her about the crazy parties she attended earlier in the semester with Zee and her friends. She just knew her story to this point was all grace. She felt really proud of her achievements, and she remembered her father's laughter upon hearing her result. He said, "My beloved daughter, I am super proud of you." She was already making some major decisions about the next semester that she wouldn't go to any more of those crazy parties, and she would get to be more consistent with her Christian book club because she learned a lot from them. She was now getting closer to their home, and she knew her mom must have outdone herself, cooking all delicacies. She would let herself bask in the praises and eat a full plate of food after a warm bath. This holiday was already looking like fun.

Train up a child in the way she should go
and when she is old, she won't depart from it.
(Proverbs 22:6)

Ronke

It was 9:00 p.m. The ambulance siren filled the air. Ade had slumped on his bathroom floor. Ade was a handsome, faithful believer in Christ Jesus. He was only fifty and was diagnosed with end-stage kidney failure. His kidneys started failing. Immediately, his son, Samuel, was born. He had done a couple of rounds of dialysis, and he had gotten worse.

Twenty years ago, Ade met, courted, and married his beloved wife, Ronke. Theirs was the perfect story of love. Ade was working for a chicken company as a manager, and Ronke was finishing up her teacher's training course at a teacher's training school. After their marriage, they had gone ahead and rented a two-bedroom apartment and walking in faith furnished one of the rooms as the nursery, filling it with all gender-neutral colors.

The first five years of married life passed, and the highly anticipated baby didn't come. They prayed and sowed financial seeds, yet it didn't happen. The nursery started becoming a reminder of all they desired which wasn't yet available in real life. They kept believing.

Days became weeks, and weeks turned into months, then months to years. They visited all the renowned fertility clinics and were pronounced clinically healthy, yet they had unprotected copulation for these years without fruits to show for it. This was actually primary infertility.

Ade's mother visited often with some local herb concoction and encouraged Ronke to drink it daily as this will smoothen the uterus and also activate quick fertilization. The couple attended every conference, prayer meeting, deliverance service, and miracle summit which helped their faith.

Ade and Ronke were a ride-or-die couple. They weathered storms which came from supposed friends and the society at large, those nosy types who start counting the time for conception immediately after the wedding and say things like, "Are you planning on having kids at all?" "Ronke, don't tell me you are still fitting into your size 6 gowns?" "The prices of formula and diapers are increasing. Better start having them sooner than later." They both answered with a smile and positive words. They hoped and kept each other going.

One Father's Day, at a chicken factory, they had shared tickets to the soccer game with all the fathers, and Ade got none. When he questioned the HR, she answered unapologetically in her shrill voice, "Well, Mr. Ade, you are not yet a father." This hurt Ade's feelings a lot, and he talked to his wife about it. They hugged and sobbed together.

One day, Ronke got really sick and decided to see her doctor on getting to the hospital. The doctor sent her to the laboratory to run some tests. It included a pregnancy test, and to the glory of God, Ronke was pronounced pregnant after seventeen years of marriage. There was unending joy in the family of Mr. and Mrs. Ade Gbenga. Ronke continued to work at the secondary school where she secured a job immediately after graduation from the teacher's training college and really took it easy. She took all her vitamins, mostly folic acid. She attended all her doctor's appointments and prayers in church for expectant mothers. Her ultrasound revealed a healthy baby boy. The couple cried for joy. This was a miracle. The sonographer asked if this was their first. They both replied *yes*, and Ronke thought, *If only this sonographer lady knew all we have been through.*

On her third trimester, she took time off work as the ultrasound also revealed that the placenta was positioned very close to the delivery canal. She was going to be scheduled for a cesarean section. She was seen by a fetal specialist who confirmed this and agreed with the obstetrics and gynecology doctor that Ronke shouldn't be allowed to go into labor as that would result in hemorrhage which will result in maternal and fetal mortality.

On the scheduled day, Ade and his pregnant wife came into the women's and children's unit holding hands and trusting God. Ronke went through all the preoperative procedures with Ade gallantly by her side every step of the way. The surgery was successful, and Ronke delivered a two-pound-and-three-ounce bundle of great joy. He was the light of their world from that day. They named him Samuel.

Samuel grew in health and was dedicated when he was three months old. The Gbengas' joy was full. Finally, that nursery which was fast becoming a storage room, and the visitor's room was now occupied by a real baby. Friends and family came in their numbers to rejoice with them and of course, the others to see if it was true.

Ade started noticing that he was having decreased urine output, swelling in his legs, ankles, and feet, and shortness of breath. He consulted a renal specialist as directed by his primary physician and he was diagnosed with acute kidney failure. The couple was shaken by the news but drew their strength from knowing that some patients got better after a couple of rounds of dialysis. The doctor said some patients' kidneys picked up and started functioning after treatment and dialysis.

They drew their strength from their young, thriving son. Ronke's sister, Tolu, had to come and help the couple out as she just finished her WAEC (West African Examination Council) board. Tolu tended to Samuel while Ade and Ronke started going in for dialysis appointments. He was both bottle- and breast-fed at this time. The dialysis made Ade tired and became leaner as the years progressed. Ade's kidneys never returned to normal.

Sam was two years now. He was running around his parents' room, and Ronke could hear Ade telling him to quit playing with his shoes as they were dirty. She was making dinner and deep in thought about how faith in God was not actually an exemption from the vicissitudes of life. Rather, we are promised that God goes with us, through thick and thin.

Tolu passed her JAMB (Joint Admissions and Matriculations Board) last year and gained admission into the University of Port Harcourt to study theatre arts. She had gone back to school. Ronke counted her blessings—a husband who loved her through their trying time (He never put her down or made her feel less. They carried their infertility burden till she become a mother), a wonderful, quick-witted son, and all the support she needed from their extended family. Then came Sam, he said, "Mommy, Mommy," and started pulling his mom to follow him to where Daddy was. Ronke obliged him. Thinking it was one of his demands. She got to the room and didn't see Ade. She felt this dread when she screamed his name, and he didn't answer. She looked in the bathroom and saw her husband sprawled on the floor. She was livid with fear. She immediately called 911, and they sent an ambulance. It was a quick response.

At the hospital, the doctor who revived Ade came out to inform Ronke that her husband was doing as well as one with his diagnosis and got better after a couple of weeks of being admitted. The doctor suggested it was best to transfer him to hospice because his health had really deteriorated. It was still a rude shock to Ronke even though she saw this coming. She thought they still had more time. Her sweetheart, hero, and love of her life was slipping fast.

Ronke's family and Ade's family have been constantly there for them, and Ronke's mother took care of Sam most of the time while Ronke spent time with her dying husband. She didn't want to miss a moment, and that day came when Ade said to Ronke, "Please let me go, my love. Draw comfort from our promise fulfilled by God, our young son." He had made good financial plans that will keep them comfortable.

Then in tears, Ronke said those words, "I know, my love, that you are leaving this sick body to be with our Lord. We will meet and will never part again. I will forever tell our son how great you are, and I would never remarry again." Ade told her to please remarry if she should find love again. She refused that, then in the evening of that day, Ade gave up to the Ghost. Ronke screamed and called the nurses and doctors. He had signed against any forms of resuscitation, and he had his DNR band on.

Ronke's hero, her ride-or-die, her strong side lay there lifeless. She drew strength from knowing he was in a better place. It didn't make that stab-like pain in her heart go away, but it gave her the strength to take the next step toward home. As she got home, she held her sleeping son, and tears descended like streams.

> He keeps in perfect peace all whose eyes
> are stayed on him because their trust is in him.
> (Isaiah 26:3)

Obiadada

"Nkoli, bring us more palm wine!" screamed Obi. Uche and Ebuka had come to visit as usual. They never lost the excitement of catching up on any events that had happened during their day. Obi was a devout Christian. He had fully accepted Christ and made sure all his family members also did. His son, Emeka, was attending a Methodist school. He still took palm wine which he made sure was fresh and taken in moderation. He was still working on that habit.

His chieftaincy ceremony was in a week. He had lived all his life trusting that one day he will be established. He was a good provider for his family, a man of character, and a trusted warrior. His theme always was for every young man and woman to be hardworking and kind to everyone both rich and poor, for you never know what tomorrow holds for everyone. When his friends left, Obi sat still and, his past all came like a flood

Obiadada was a boy again in his thoughts, and he had run off with his mother to his maternal grandmother's, and his father had come with his kinsmen to ensure they came back home. His parents had a fight which resulted in Obi and his mother, Mma, leaving their home. Obi's father, Ike, was very poor, so poor that the poor called him poor. They had a roof over their head and had plenty during the yam season. Once that season passed, it was back to poverty till the next season. Mma had to work extra to grow perishable food and sell it to feed Obi and his siblings, and she had about had it. The meeting went well, and the family was reunited.

Obi looked at the state of his family and vowed to fight poverty with all he had. He attended his school to learn basic communication and calculation skills. Once he was old enough, his father could not afford to put him through secondary school. He quickly went to live with his uncle Uba to learn large-scale planting and trading food products to the north and also harvesting crops from the north to sell them in the other regions of the country. He learned this and became very successful when he completed the period of learning under his uncle. He later met his friends, Uche and Ebuka, who were also involved in this trade. Each was selling small scale. They decided to form a partnership, pull their funds together, and form a strong partnership for large-scale production and sales.

Their partnership prospered greatly. They started getting married, and each had children. Then Obiadada knew how families can have problems, and it would affect the working relationship of friends. He then called his friends and proposed that they part in peace and divide their wealth equally, to prevent any grudges or messy breakups in the future. His friends disagreed with his idea for a while then went on with it. These thoughts made Obi smile. They were all in a good place because they made that decision. They were still good friends, doing well in their pursuits, though Obi was the most successful of the three.

Obi thought of all the families who called them poor back in the days; now he was building houses for them. Funny how life can change. There's a saying that we should be kind to people we meet on our way up because we might just need them on our way down. The Lord had chosen to honor his effort and to bless the works of his hands. Clearly the case of the stone which the builders rejected become the chief cornerstone. The same boy whose family was not recognized at all was being ushered into the most prestigious office of a chief with sheer hard work, faith in God, and focus.

His farm work and trade flourished so much that he was a very good provider to his family, and he was training a son in a Methodist school. His greatest joy and fulfillment was his stable family. Nkoli had always brought him such favor and joy together with their lovely three children, Emeka, Unoaku, and Cheta. Unoaku was growing into a very brilliant and beautiful young woman of which Obi was proud. She was in the school for textile designers. She made lovely tie-dye clothing for her parents. She would be joining Emeka at the Methodist secondary school later in the year.

Obi made up his mind to ensure his children learned some skills alongside academics. Cheta was still in primary school doing great with his grammar and numbers. Obi lived a life of gratitude. That was his greatest key, for he never focused on his problems. He came up with solutions to tackle his problems, but he stayed thankful. He had made up his mind to have a peaceful home free of rancor and to have a joyful wife. He achieved it. He didn't like the entirety of what his parents modeled to him. He simply picked the good and tried his best through prayers and a strong resolve to avoid reliving the bad.

Nkoli came in and called her husband. That brought him back from his reverie. They had to go and do their final fitting at the tailor's and get theirs and their children's clothes back home in readiness for the big day. Nkoli was godly and demure, and she was loved by all who knew her, who better to be the chief's wife. She would play her role to her people as she had diligently served her family no doubt. Obi smiled on seeing the concern on her face. She worried a lot. She wanted everything to be just perfect. Obi held her hand and reassured her. They left for the tailors laughing as Obi displayed the new dance steps he had planned for his chieftaincy ceremony.

> The stone the builders rejected has become
> the chief cornerstone. (Psalm 118:22)

Uwem

It was too late for Uwem to be coming home; Adanne had had enough. She was done with Uwem's unrealistic outlook on life. "Come on, young man," she said. "Put your head down. Study and make something of your life. The looks will fade one day. You won't look that tall forever. You can't base your life off your handsome look." Uwem was coming back to Adanne's family house at twelve midnight. He was from his numerous night parties. He couldn't keep up with paying his rent, so he moved in with his sister, and her family in the meantime as he said. Uwem was not just the only son. He had five sisters. He was that child who was pampered and given privileges. Now what? He lacked the ability to make gainful choices for his life, and when anyone wanted to advise him, he talked them out. He was a good orator. He would list out plans from the top of his head. These plans changed every single time. That was why everyone knew he wasn't working toward meeting any of them.

Uwem had secured admission into one of the most prestigious universities. He achieved this amid his parents' and sisters' pleas and immense support. Now it was time to go on and study economics which he applied for, and he started procrastinating. Adanne knew he was so intelligent, and he will do well if only he'd pull his head out of the cloud and focus on making something of his life. He never took the word *time* into consideration. He was handsome and living what he viewed as his best life. The two sales agents who worked with Jaja (Adanne's husband) envied him and often told lies against him saying he took money from the customers and didn't account for it. Jaja never confronted Uwem about it.

Madam Deola was a well-renowned widow who enjoyed the company of younger men. Her numerous society lady friends threw her a grand fifty birthday party, and Uwem attended with one of his former high school buddies. Immediately Madam Deola saw Uwem. She said she fell head over heels in love and sought to reach him through his friend who was a mutual friend. This was the worst thing that ever happened to Uwem. He was already a scatter head.

He hit it off with Madam Deola. They partied every night. He moved into her lovely home. Life was beautiful or seemingly so for dear Uwem. He hardly had time for his family, who would call a million times and leave him tons of messages. He declined his admission and continued to live in his fool's paradise.

Years passed and Madam Deola's fancy for her boyfriend started to seriously wane. There was a new catch. They started getting into more and more quarrels, and like a flash of lightning the relationship ended, and Uwem was devastated. He moved back to his sister's home, and she received him like the father of the prodigal son. Uwem resumed helping out with sales at Jaja's confectionary and trying to move on after the breakup. Adanne never bothered to discuss it. When she was home she was mostly busy with her two young children, Keke and Pam. Uwem was at a loss as to what he really wanted to achieve in life. He took an interest finally in the baking unit at the confectionary, and things started looking up for him. He was so creative that he baked the most artistic cakes which tasted like heaven.

Ten years later, Uwem had lost so much weight. He had been getting ill a lot and feeding off over-the-counter cold and cough mixtures. Then this particular day, Adanne, whose kids were now teenagers, had a lot of free time on her hands. She pressed Uwem into going to the hospital. They did, and the doctor sent them to run tests and called them in when the results were sent to him. He smiled, and Adanne could tell something was wrong. He asked if Uwem lived alone, and there were quite other little chitchats asking how many people made contact with Uwem every day. Then he finally cut to the chase. He asked Uwem if it was alright for me to hear his laboratory result, and Uwem answered in the affirmative. The doctor asked if they have heard about AIDS.

"We had heard so little about it back then. We told him the little we knew, and he further enlightened us about HIV and AIDS." He then released the bombshell that Uwem had AIDS. It was the hardest thing. It felt like a death sentence. They were both in shock. Adanne asked questions about the options of treatment which was met with none. They went home and made the appropriate arrangements. Adanne rented an apartment for her brother, and their mom came to live with Uwem. He became sicker in the coming weeks. He had rashes all over his body and had constant diarrhea. He was weaker and really lean now. The friends who partied with him were nowhere to be found. His family rallied around him and loved him till he took his last breath.

Uwem was buried in a cemetery. The arrangements were made by Jaja and Uwem's uncle. Adanne was traveling for her work assignment. She went berserk when she returned and heard what happened.

She screamed at Jaja, "You wouldn't even let me say goodbye to my only brother. Oh, not even a proper goodbye." She cried and mourned for her only brother for a long time.

There is a way that seems right unto a man
but its end is death. (Proverbs 14:12)

Sade

Sade was the typical Ugly Betty or so she was told by society. They'd say, "Sade, your face is not right. Your nose is too big. your complexion is not just right. Your lips are just too wide. Your eyes are too small. Your legs are too thin. You have broad shoulders and really long arms." She was told by everyone around her she just wasn't good enough, but Sade had this strong belief in who the Lord said she was. She had received Christ early in her life, and that framed her thoughts about herself. No matter what anyone said, she was fighting to have healthy esteem without even knowing what she was doing, no matter what was great or not about her features. She told herself, "God is good, and all he creates is good." She called herself loved and accepted as the Lord called her. She had gone to a really low-standard school and had failed her final senior secondary exam. She was taken to live with her mother's sister, Aunty Bose, and her family to attend her senior class again and write the exam again.

Aunty Bose had an interesting family. She lost her husband after a sudden heart attack some years ago, so she ran her home with her set of rules. Wake up early at 5:00 a.m., pray, clean up, and rush to the restaurant which was a walk away to join the two cooks to start cooking and serving the early risers and early workers, mostly breakfast menu like eggs, toast, bacon, grit, hot dogs, oatmeal, tea, or coffee. Her aunt ran the local restaurant which all the members of the community patronized. Sade had to leave halfway through the morning service and craziness to head to school after taking a bite. She kept her eyes on her purpose.

Her teachers in this new school were vested in ensuring all the students were well acquainted with the study materials. After school, Sade would return to the restaurant and wash her hands then join the afternoon routine. They made fried beef and chicken, mashed potatoes, fries, okra, pounded yam, fried and boiled yam, softly boiled vegetables, and rice of different types ranging from white rice with sauce to jollof rice to fried rice, depending on which day of the week it was. The afternoons were busier. Lots of workers would come in for their lunch break.

Sade didn't just serve her aunty and the numerous customers at the restaurant. Her aunty made sure she ran errands for her children, Demi and Ayo. This was a lot for young Sade, but she was a survivor, and she kept her eyes on the price—to finish school, pass her senior secondary exam, get a job, and move out. Annoyingly she noticed Ayomide would touch her carelessly lately, and she didn't want to sound insulting by calling him out or being seen as one who had such evil thoughts, but she knew she wasn't imagining things.

Then thankfully, she saved up from the little tips they share in the kitchen and paid for her senior secondary exams. She studied against all odds, and the three weeks of the exam came, and she passed. The results would be out in another month. To the glory of God, Sade didn't just pass; she was one of the best. Sade constantly sent letters to her mom and kept her abreast on new happenings. She did her best to keep it positive. Another good news was that with Aunty Bose's permission, Sade got employed at the cement factory as the company clerk.

Little did she know she had carried all that skunk from her past, and when she felt the lies about her body coming as thoughts and voices in her head more than normal now. She became more intentional about fighting this battle in her mind. She began speaking back to stop them. She wrote healthy love notes to herself. Then she prayed and meditated, she took time to recount and be grateful for all the Lord had blessed her. She began reading healthy books on self-love and building healthy esteem. She ate right. She moved out of Aunty Bose's after thanking her immensely with some presents in hand. Immediately, she earned her first salary. She continued to allow herself to love herself as Christ loved her and tried to be the best version of herself.

Then one day in November started as just like any other day. She never knew it was going to change her life for good. She came into work with her bubblegum-pink formal dress with her fuchsia pink and black scarf. She was a sight for sore eyes. She was so busy getting her tasks completed for the day being a Thursday. She had to clear her table before the weekend. While she was on it, a young man walked in and asked to see her boss. She greeted kindly and directed him to sit while she contacted the boss's secretary, and in a couple of minutes, she called him in to see the boss.

Months later, the same young man came back for a meeting, and then formally introduced himself as Kingsley. He asked Sade out on a lunch break, and from there, they hit it off. They exchanged numbers and didn't go a day without communicating the highs and the lows of their day. Kingsley was a man of faith too. It worked in his favor because they prayed together. They invited each other to their place of worship as the weeks went by. By the second date, Kingsley knew he had found a virtuous woman. He proposed after six months, and she said *yes*. They tied the knot in Sade's church in the presence of both families. It was within the two families. How they both wanted it. Their love was so evident as they shared their written vows. The couple felt so blessed.

They had good days and bad days. They stuck together having great respect for each other. They had two boys whom they loved and raised together. Sade looked back and smiled at all they said she would never become. Indeed her faith hasn't made her ashamed. She had thrived and soared above all the negative words that were said against her and see how beautiful the Lord had made her story.

> The Lord looked at all he created and called
> them good. (Genesis 1:31)

About the Author

Elizabeth Chidumaga Emejuaiwe is a Christian author who loves to see the love of the Father flow into our day-to-day challenges and culture helping us live fuller and more peaceful lives as we yield to our Father's will for our lives. Her whole passion is to, with the help of the Holy Spirit, resound the message of the Lord Jesus to all, saying we are loved by the Father. This book is a Kingdom Evangelism tool.

She has a bachelor's degree in nursing from the University of Port Harcourt, Nigeria. She started her nursing practice in Nigeria and has continued to serve abroad.

She is married, and they are blessed with a child.